"I didn't want this book to end! It's funny and exciting, and I enjoyed every page."
—Yoni Lefkowits, 9

"This is a fantastic book, with a lot of humor. The ending is so surprising, you would never expect it!"
—Yaakov Krauss, 13

"I loved this book! Having a workshop to invent things in is such a cool idea! I wish I had that too!"
—Simchi Traube, 11

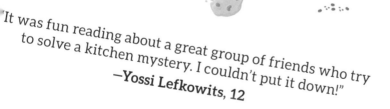

"It was fun reading about a great group of friends who try to solve a kitchen mystery. I couldn't put it down!"
—Yossi Lefkowits, 12

CHAOS IN THE KITCHEN

MENUCHA PUBLISHERS

The Super Sleuth Trio

CHAOS IN THE KITCHEN

Sara Sumner

Menucha Publishers, Inc.
© 2021 by Sara Summer

Typeset and designed by Deena Weinberg

ISBN 978-1-61465-561-9
Library of Congress Control Number: 2021935421

Published and distributed by:
Menucha Publishers, Inc.
1235 38th Street
Brooklyn, NY 11218
Tel/Fax: 718-232-0856
www.menuchapublishers.com

Printed in Israel

Drop cap letters by Macrovector/Freepik.com
Chocolate drip design by Freepik.com

TO YY,
My boy in a gaggle of girls

TO ALL MY READERS,
Discover your gifts and use them to make the world better.

CONTENTS

CHAPTER 1

SEVEN-LAYER CAKE

"Quick! Pass me another piece of tape," Yaakov called from the top of the ladder.

Yitz pulled on the roll, but when the familiar sound of ripping tape stopped too soon, he blurted, "Uh-oh!"

"What do you mean? 'Uh-oh?'" asked Yaakov.

Avi tightened his grip on the bottom of the ladder as it wobbled slightly. "Why did we agree to do this?"

Rummaging through the bag, Yitz pulled out a new roll of tape. "My sisters promised us free samples."

Yaakov smacked his lips. "Mmm, chocolate cake dripping with fudge icing."

Yitz tugged at the end of the tape, his mouth watering.

Beside him, Avi let go of the ladder to rub his tummy. "Whoops!" he said as the ladder leaned, then tipped. Yaakov tumbled to the ground, toppling Yitz.

Yaakov rolled off Yitz, laughing and holding his knee with one hand and half of the Bais Yaakov Bake Sale sign with the other. The other half of the sign was stuck to the tree.

Yitz was flat on his back, his yarmulke in the bushes behind him, and his face as red as a slice of gefilte fish smothered in *chrein*. "Can't you stay focused for even one minute?"

Avi shuffled his feet, looking at the floor.

Yitz stood up and brushed grass and pebbles off his black pants. He retrieved his yarmulke and took a step toward Avi. "Every single time, you cause a disaster! Look at my pants. Look at that sign. How can we get the job done with you like this?"

Yaakov placed a hand on Yitz's shoulder. "Come on, Yitz. It was an accident. He didn't mean to."

Yitz spun around, pulling himself out from under Yaakov's arm. "You always take his side. This is nuts," he said. "For once, can't you admit that Avi is worse than a tornado?"

Avi bit his lip and took a step toward Yitz, his eyes blazing.

Yaakov looked from one to the other and placed a calming hand on Avi's arm. Sagging, Avi took three steps back.

"I'm sorry, okay?" Avi huffed. "Let's get back to work so we can *all* get some cake."

Yitz took a deep breath and bent to pick up the ladder. "Fine. But I'm holding the ladder, and you're on tape duty from now on."

CHAPTER 2

FRUIT-FILLED CUPCAKES

"That's the last of them," Yaakov said as he folded the ladder and grasped it under his arm.

Avi whooped. "Let's go get some cake!"

Yitz clapped his two friends on the back. Together, the three of them left the cheder parking lot and began the short walk to Yitz's house.

When they arrived at the Levine house, Mr. Levine was seated on the front porch with a

Fruit-Filled Cupcakes

Chumash in his hand. "Hey, boys! Got all the posters up okay?"

"Piece of cake," said Avi.

"Easy as pie," said Yitz.

"Smooth as silken tofu ice cream," said Yaakov.

Both Avi and Yitz spun to stare at their friend. "What?" asked Yitz.

"Huh?" said Avi.

Yaakov shrugged. "Savta always makes it for Shabbos."

Mr. Levine laughed. "I can see what's on your mind."

"The girls promised samples if we hung up their signs," Yitz said.

"And we did," Yaakov said.

"So now we're here to collect," Avi said, rubbing his belly.

"Well, you can go on in there, but I don't think they have any samples ready yet." Mr. Levine leaned toward the boys and glanced both ways before lowering his voice. "Actually, I wouldn't advise going in there unless absolutely necessary. The *girls* have taken over again."

Behind Yitz, Yaakov and Avi stepped down from the porch. Yitz shuddered.

Chaos in the Kitchen

"We can come back tomorrow," said Yaakov. "Better not to get in their way."

Avi glanced at his watch. "Yeah. It's getting late. Maybe another time—"

"Come on, guys! Where's your courage?" Yitz turned to face his friends. "We did what we were asked. It's time to collect payment. *Lo talin pe'ulas sachir.* It's a mitzvah to pay your workers on time!"

Mr. Levine frowned. "Now, Yitz, I'm not sure the Torah meant chocolate cake. Give the girls a chance to make something before you demand payment."

"Maybe we should go to my house instead?" Avi asked, shifting from one foot to the other.

Yitz shook his head and pushed open the door.

With a sigh, Yaakov followed, with Avi trailing behind him.

"Chaya Bracha?" Yitz called as he kicked off his shoes in the direction of the front hall closet. "Rivkie? Malkie?"

Avi sniffed. "Looks like your father was right. No scent of dessert."

"But I can hear the buzz of too many girls... The sound's coming from the dining room," Yaakov said.

Fruit-Filled Cupcakes

"Let's check the kitchen first," Yitz said, leading the way through the small hallway and into the kitchen. He had taken just three steps into the kitchen when he fell to the ground for the second time that day.

"Oy! Are you okay?" Yaakov asked.

As Yitz rolled from his stomach to his back and propped himself up on his elbows, he watched his two friends. Yaakov bent down and picked up a doll. Beside him, Avi was trying to keep himself from laughing, pressing his lips tightly together, and blood rushing to his cheeks.

"It isn't funny."

Yaakov and Avi exchanged a look. "Yeah, it is," said Avi.

Yitz leapt up and charged at Avi. The two fell to the floor, knocking over Yaakov. When Mr. Levine came in to check out the noise just moments later, he found the three of them rolling on the floor laughing.

With a shake of the head, Mr. Levine stepped over Yitz, skirted around Yaakov, and headed out the back door to his shed.

"Shall we go find the girls and get our cake?" Yaakov asked, tossing the doll onto the table.

Chaos in the Kitchen

Avi kicked a toy stroller out of the kitchen toward the front door, while Yitz pushed his little sister's tea set into a corner.

The squealing coming from the dining room sounded even louder than usual. Yitz was used to the chatter of his sisters, but this was far worse than normal. He stuck his head out of the kitchen and peeked into the dining room. First Avi, and then Yaakov, leaned around him until three floating heads filled the doorway.

There were too many girls to count. Everywhere were more braids and skirts and ribbons and the high-pitched giggles of a gaggle of girls. The boys gasped before pulling back into the kitchen.

"We—"

"—Cannot—"

"—Go in there!"

Yaakov turned to Yitz. "Who are all those girls?"

Yitz shrugged. "I guess my sisters invited friends."

Avi shook his head, then shuddered. "It'll be safer at my house."

CHAPTER 3

CHOCOLATE CHIP COKIES

Before leaving Yitz's place, Avi called ahead to warn his mom that they were coming. Not only did she have milk and cookies set out for them on the kitchen table when they arrived, but she made sure to make herself and all his annoying little siblings scarce so the boys could have time to themselves.

There was only one issue: the cookies were burnt, and the milk was warmish (and not in an

"I can't sleep" soothing warm milk sort of way, more in an "I forgot the milk on the counter after breakfast and it's been there ever since" sort of way).

Yaakov crumbled a cookie, eating only the chocolate chips and stuffing a napkin with the charred crumbs. "Are you ready for the big Chumash test next week?"

Yitz shook his head. "How am I supposed to remember all the commentaries?"

"I can barely remember the basic story," said Avi, "but we'll get through it like we always do. Let's get together tomorrow after school to study."

"I'm in," Yaakov said. "Where should we meet?"

Yitz rubbed his hands together. "How 'bout my house? Maybe the girls will have started baking and we can get our samples."

"*Mmm*, maybe they'll have apple pie," Avi said.

"Or lemon meringue pie," said Yitz.

"Or chicken pot pie," Yaakov said.

Avi grabbed some crumbs from the table and tossed them at Yaakov. "That's not dessert!"

Yaakov shrugged. "Doesn't mean it isn't yummy."

CHAPTER 4

HOT TAMALES

itz slammed the door and headed straight for the kitchen. His stomach rumbled. Meatloaf night was one of his favorite nights of the week. "Mom? When's dinner?"

The only response was a chorus of squeals. "No boys."

"Don't come in here."

"Leave us alone or we'll never get our baking started."

Chaos in the Kitchen

"I live here, too, you know," Yitz said, standing in the doorway.

Rivkie took a step toward him and blocked the entrance. "But you'll only be in the way."

"Where's Mom?" Yitz asked, taking a step toward Rivkie in response.

"Putting the little ones to bed," Malkie said.

Rivkie placed her hands on her hips, standing her ground. "Maybe you should go there, too."

"I'm eleven months older than you. If anyone needs bed, it's clearly you," Yitz said.

Another step, and Rivkie was right in his face. They stood toe-to-toe in the doorway, trapped in a staring contest. No matter what happened, Yitz would never blink first.

Yitz leaned forward. He clenched his fists at his side. His mouth turned down in a frown. And still, he would not blink. Rivkie had no right to stop him from going through parts of his own house. A small growl escaped his lips.

Rivkie smirked and stuck out her tongue. "This week, this is our kitchen, and you are not allowed in."

"Why don't you take your whiny voice and your silly head and—"

Hot Tamales

But no one found out where Rivkie should take it all, because a hand clamped down on Yitz's shoulder, stopping him mid-sentence. Startled, Yitz spun around to find his father standing there. Mr. Levine smiled at Yitz, ignoring the fight.

"Come on, Yitz, we have a shopping list to attend to, and these girls need to get baking. Why don't you and I head to the store and grab something for dinner?"

Yitz let out a breath and shook his head. "Why should I do anything for them?"

Mr. Levine squeezed Yitz's shoulder. "You aren't. You're doing it for me."

With a backward glare at his sisters, Yitz trudged out of the house after his father.

CHAPTER 5

HOLEY COKIES

r. Levine took Yitz to Pizza Palace and ordered them a large pie with extra cheese and two sodas. The girls always insisted on vegetable toppings like tomatoes and peppers, and his mother always said pizza was enough of a treat, so no one needed more than water. That night, because it was only the guys, they got to do pizza right.

Honey Cookies

"Mommy told the girls they need to be more organized tomorrow so she can get into the kitchen to make supper in addition to their baking," his father said.

Yitz nodded and stirred his cola with his straw. He didn't say anything. Meatloaf was delicious, but there was nothing better than pizza. Around them, the shop was filling up with fathers and sons from the community. Yitz wasn't the only one thrown out of his kitchen in honor of the Bais Yaakov Bake Sale. Mr. Levine noticed it, too. "Looks like we have lots of company for dinner tonight," he said.

Yitz shifted in his seat. His fight with his sisters was still bothering him. "Why are girls allowed to throw us out like this? It isn't fair that I can never feel comfortable in my own home."

Mr. Levine nodded. "I know you're upset. This is one more time when it's really tough to be an only son, but at least I have one ally, right?"

Yitz shrugged and took a bite of his pizza.

"You know, there's a saying, 'You catch more bees with honey.' Do you understand what it means?"

Yitz shrugged again. "I guess it means honey is sweet and bees like it, so you'll get more."

Mr. Levine smiled. "Good. But, so what?"

Yitz picked at his cheese.

"Yitz, sometimes I get so angry I want to scream. But part of growing up and getting to be a daddy is learning to control that."

Yitz looked up and met his father's eyes. "You get angry like that?"

Mr. Levine nodded. "Sometimes I have a troublemaking son who hits a baseball through the kitchen window, breaking not only the window but also all the dishes in the sink."

Blushing, Yitz hid behind his cola. "I didn't mean to."

Mr. Levine laughed. "Oh, I know, and actually it takes a certain amount of talent to cause that much trouble. But it doesn't mean at the time I didn't want to have a temper tantrum like Chavie does."

Peeking up at his father, Yitz tried to understand. "But you didn't scream. You told Avi and me to clean up the mess and make sure we apologized to Mommy."

"That's because I have worked really hard to

control that part of me. We all get angry. I'm not saying it's easy. Because it isn't. But back to those bees. If I try to grab them with force, it would be really hard. Chances are, I'll get stung. But what do we do in the sukkah?"

"We have that trap that lets them in but not out."

"Right. We put some honey in the middle of it. It draws them in. Honey makes bees easy to catch."

Yitz scratched his head with his yarmulke. "So, you're saying..."

"If you lash out at your sisters, they very well may sting you. Maybe a different tactic will get you more of what you want?"

Quietly, Yitz chewed on his father's words while he chewed his pizza. Honey. Could he switch to honey?

CHAPTER 6

SUGAR BROWNIES

"Smells like dessert is ready and waiting," Mr. Levine said as he opened the door and took a sniff.

Yitz could smell it as well. He followed his father into the kitchen, carrying two bags of groceries. Placing the bags in the center of the floor, he looked around for the source of the sweet scent.

Chaya Bracha was the only one still in the kitchen. She was washing dishes. A tray of brownies was cooling on the counter beside her. Someone had already taken a row of slices out.

Yitz passed the garbage on the way to investigate. Far too many crumbs littered the top of the trash.

"Chaya Bracha, it looks like you already have one dessert ready," Mr. Levine said. He picked up a knife from the draining rack and waved it over the brownies. "Mind if Yitz and I try a bite?"

Turning off the water, Chaya Bracha grabbed a towel, then turned to her father. "Something isn't right with them. You can try, but they're way too sweet."

Mr. Levine cut two small squares and handed one to Yitz.

"I really don't understand," continued Chaya Bracha, "we followed the recipe exactly. But it was one we hadn't made before. Maybe the book has a typo? Although Mommy said it looked all right to her."

Shrugging, Mr. Levine made a berachah and took a bite. Yitz said "amen," then did the same.

Yitz's lips puckered as he tried to swallow the gooey, sugary concoction. He never thought he'd ever think something could be too sweet!

Chaos in the Kitchen

Mr. Levine chewed and swallowed. "I see what you mean," he said, reaching for a cup and filling it with water. "Did you use chocolate milk powder instead of cocoa?"

Chaya Bracha shook her head. "No. It can't be..." she said, trailing off. She shrugged. "Well, maybe. Rivkie was mixing the dry ingredients."

Mr. Levine opened the pantry and pointed at the tins of chocolate milk powder and cocoa on the top shelf. "Easy rookie mistake. Look, with them side by side like that, you can't always tell the difference."

Yitz smirked. He liked the idea of Rivkie messing up. "What are you going to do with the brownies?"

Chaya Bracha glanced at the tray and shrugged. "I'm not sure."

Grabbing his own cup of water, Yitz wandered over to the table and sat down. He alternated between small bites of brownie and large gulps of water, while his sister and father continued to talk.

"Maybe you could use them as a crust for a dessert for Shabbos?" Mr. Levine suggested.

"That's a good idea. I'll put it in the freezer for now and let Mommy know in the morning."

"Well, with that all settled, I have groceries to bring in and put away," said Mr. Levine, looking meaningfully at Yitz.

Jumping up from the chair, Yitz took one more bite of his brownie and found he couldn't eat anymore. He tossed it in the garbage pail. As Chaya Bracha turned back to the sink of dishes, Yitz followed his father to the car.

CHAPTER 7

ELEPHANT EARS

vi, Yaakov, and Yitz walked home together nearly every day. So when Avi took off at a run as soon as they got out of class, Yaakov and Yitz grabbed their bags and ran after him.

"Hey, Avi," Yaakov called, "wait up!"

Always the fastest of the three, Yitz caught up easily and grabbed Avi's backpack, pulling his friend to a stop. "Why'd you run off?" he asked. "I thought we decided you were coming to my house to study."

Avi straightened his yarmulke and shifted back and forth as if he were getting ready to run again. Yitz tightened his grip on Avi's bag as Yaakov came huffing up to them.

"You know my legs aren't as long as yours. Why didn't you wait for me?"

Yitz turned to Avi. "I don't know. Ask him."

"Maybe I don't want to study with two boring slow pokes like you anyway."

Yitz let go of Avi's bag and stepped back as if he'd been slapped. "What's gotten into you?"

Avi shrugged. "There's somewhere I've got to be. And you're holding me up."

Yaakov stepped between his two friends. "Come on, guys, what's going on here?"

Yitz squeezed his hands into fists. Like a kettle about to whistle, he felt heat simmering. Then he thought of pizza and his father and bees and honey. What would his father want him to do? He took a deep breath and tried again. "Avi, the girls will be baking. I'm sure they'll have something for us to try. We never got paid for yesterday."

And, amazingly, it worked. Yitz felt like someone had pulled the plug on his kettle, and beside him, Avi went from glaringly angry to awkwardly shy.

Avi dug into the grass with his toe. "Mommy said I need to get home straight after school today. I— I—"

"You have a doctor's appointment?" Yaakov asked.

"Nah."

"We really wanted you to come. Maybe you can call her from my house and see if you could stay for just a little?"

Avi shook his head and bit his lip. He looked like he wanted to say more but then shook his head. "Ask them to save me a piece, okay?"

Yitz nodded.

Yaakov stepped toward Avi like he was going to push further, but before either of them could stop him, Avi hiked up his back-pack, turned, and ran off down the street. Too startled to chase him again, Yitz watched him until he turned the corner and was out of sight.

Elephant Ears

"What do you think that was about?" Yaakov asked.

Yitz shrugged. He didn't always get along so well with Avi, but without him there, it felt like their tripod was missing a leg and the camera was about to fall over. "Let's go, Yaakov. We have tons of studying to do."

CHAPTER 8

DEVIL'S FOD CAKE

r. Serious — Yaakov — sat, back straight and eyes completely focused on his notebook, at Yitz's two-person desk. He had shoved Yitz's deck of cards, his Lego space station, and comic book stack to one side, and spread out his notes, Chumash, and dictionary in front of him.

Behind him, sprawled on his mostly made

bed, Yitz tossed a tape ball into the air and caught it. "What does Rashi say?" Yitz asked, tossing the ball again.

The toss was a little off. The ball ended up hitting the wall, rebounding off the window, and landing with a squishy sound on Yaakov's Chumash. In a huff, Yaakov flicked the ball to the side, where it rolled off the desk and under Chavie's crib.

"Great. Now I won't find it until Pesach cleaning."

"Good," Yaakov shot back, "then maybe we can get some studying done until then."

Yitz sat up and grumbled, "It's the smell! I can't concentrate."

Yaakov closed his eyes and sniffed the air. He shrugged, then turned back to his books. Yitz stared at his friend in shock. How could he work like this? The heavenly aroma of chocolate cake fresh from the oven made Yitz dizzy. The scent had been growing stronger over the last half hour, first creeping under the door and tickling his nose. Now the smell filled every corner of the room, until it smelled better than his birthday cake, or even a bakery cake on erev Shabbos, or even a bakery cake on erev Shabbos when it was his birthday and his father was letting him choose *anything* he wanted from the store.

Yaakov sighed, then closed and kissed his Chumash. "We'd better go get you some of that cake if we're going to get anything done."

Yitz whooped and jumped up from his bed. "Let's go collect our due!" He smacked his lips.

Yaakov rolled his eyes but nodded and raced Yitz down the stairs to the kitchen. At the foot of the stairs, Yaakov tripped over a mini pink teacup filled with murky water. He hit the ground before Yitz could grab him.

"I'm okay," he said, jumping up. "But ew! What's all over my hands?"

Yitz brushed tiny white crystals from his friend's knees as Yaakov wiped it off his hands. Shrugging, Yitz stepped over the abandoned tea party and into the kitchen. "I smell payment," he said.

Inside, his sisters giggled. "Right on time, Yitz," Rivkie said.

Malkie nodded. "We wondered how long we

would have to wait for you to get here."

Yitz rubbed his belly, eyeing the large, square, and perfectly moist chocolate cake cooling on the counter. "We're working hard up there. We deserve a break," he said.

Yaakov licked his lips, then slid into the closest seat at the table.

The girls laughed again. Rivkie carried two tall glasses of milk to the table, while Malkie began to slice the cake. "We may have more posters for you to hang up," Malkie said over her shoulder.

Yitz jumped into the chair across from Yaakov. "If that cake tastes as good as it looks and smells, anything you want."

With a flourish, Malkie placed the cake before the boys as Rivkie returned with two forks.

Yaakov looked at his plate and grinned. "Avi doesn't know what he's missing."

"Bon appétit," the girls chorused.

Yitz smirked at his sisters, made a berachah, took a huge chunk of cake on his fork, and stuffed it in his mouth. He had barely closed his lips over the chocolatey dessert when the taste of the Dead

Chaos in the Kitchen

Sea flooded his mouth and invaded his taste buds.

Without a thought, he spit out the cake as quickly as he could. The now soggy chunk of cake shot straight from his lips across the table, hitting Rivkie squarely between the eyes. Yitz grabbed his milk and gulped it down. "Are you trying to poison me?" he spluttered.

"You did that on purpose," Rivkie wailed as she wiped at her chocolate-speckled forehead.

Yaakov gaped at the siblings with his own fork of cake halfway to his mouth.

"Are you insane?" Malkie asked.

By this point, Yitz was on his feet, squaring off against his sisters. "Am I insane? Are you insane? Do you think it's funny playing such a trick on us? Where's the real cake?"

Malkie stepped forward, eyes narrowed. "Do you really think we're going to fall for this? Do you really think I'll give you another piece if you pretend this one tastes bad?"

"Pretend? No one could make this up! The whole thing tastes like salt. What did you do? Coat our pieces in salt before giving them to us? Did you really think I would hang up more of your silly signs if you did something like this?

Devil's Food Cake

What is this? Revenge for our fight yesterday? Don't you think that's a little childish?"

Yaakov's fork clattered back to his plate, and he pushed his chair away from the table. He glanced at the doorway leading back to the stairs, looking for an escape.

Rivkie glared at Yitz. "You're such a baby," she said.

"I'm eleven months *older* than you!"

She placed her hands on her hips. "Well, I guess that proves girls mature faster than boys."

"You think I'm making it up? You try it," Yitz said, gesturing to Yaakov's untouched plate.

Rivkie smirked and then picked up the discarded fork. Malkie, meanwhile, broke a piece off an untouched corner of Yitz's slice.

Yitz couldn't stop from laughing as his sisters' faces turned from smug to horrified. Coughing and spluttering, they both ran to the sink to rinse out their mouths.

"How can that be?" Malkie asked. "I followed the recipe exactly."

"It smells so good. I don't understand!" Rivkie cried. Then she turned on Yitz. "What did *you* do?"

Chaos in the Kitchen

"Hey? What's that supposed to mean?"

Malkie opened the pantry and pulled out the sugar jar. Popping off the lid, she stuck her finger in, then popped the tiny crystals in her mouth. She wrinkled her nose. "Salt!"

"What?" asked Rivkie.

"What?" echoed Yitz and Yaakov.

"It's salt," Malkie said, stepping toward Yitz and waving the container. "You did this, didn't you?"

"What? Why would I mix up the sugar and salt?"

Rivkie stepped toward him and started ticking off points on her fingers. "You were mad last night. You went shopping with Daddy. You put away the groceries. You had a motive and the opportunity. It was *you*."

Yitz felt his face heat up. On either side of him, his fists clenched and unclenched as he stepped toward his sister. "Maybe *you* did it to get me in trouble."

"Oh, sure, makes a ton of sense. I said to Malkie, 'Hey, let's mess up our own cake and ruin our bake sale so we can frame Yitz.'"

"Don't expect me to understand the workings of a *girl's* mind."

Devil's Food Cake

Yaakov put a hand on Yitz's shoulder. "Come on, Yitz. Maybe it would be best to go back to your room?"

Too angry to control himself, Yitz twisted out from under Yaakov and pushed him away. "Every day. Every single day I have to put up with you girls. I'm sick of being ganged up on. I'm tired of being part of this house," he said, before storming out the back door.

Yaakov shrugged and followed him.

CHAPTER 9

CARAMEL NUT BARS

itz broke into a run and didn't stop until he reached Avi's house. By then, he had calmed down enough to see that the fight had been a little ridiculous and a lot embarrassing. Why did Yaakov have to be there to see him fighting with Rivkie and Malkie like that? The entire ten-minute run, he had ignored Yaakov's calls to stop or slow down, and by the time Yaakov came up panting beside him, Yitz had already tried the doorbell twice with no response.

"Guess he's not home," Yaakov said between gasps for breath.

"Where is he, then?"

Yaakov shrugged. "Let's go back, Yitz. I have to get my books from your house and head home anyway."

Yitz tried the bell one more time, waited, then shook his head. "Okay. We'll sneak in through the garage to avoid my *sisters*."

A loud crash coming from Mr. Levine's shed startled Yitz and Yaakov as they tried to sneak back into the house. They exchanged looks and then turned and ran to the shed.

"Is everything okay, Mr. Levine?" Yaakov asked as they peeked around the door.

In Yitz's opinion, the shed was the best room in (or out of) the house. It sat in one corner of the yard, against the tall wooden fence dividing their property from the Gordons'. Yitz's father had built the shed himself out of leftover sukkah boards and discarded sheet metal. The tin roof kept out the elements, but not the sound of rain, hail, and snow.

Although no sign hung on the slightly crooked door, everyone in the Levine household knew this space was for the men of the house — meaning Yitz and his father — only. No girls allowed. Ever.

A bare lightbulb hanging from the ceiling and a spindly table lamp provided the light. A single wall fan hung over the door to cool the tiny safe house in the summer, and an ancient space heater was nestled under his father's desk to warm it in the winter.

A floor-to-ceiling pegboard covered in hooks lined one wall, holding tools, broken picture frames, and various gizmos Mr. Levine had picked up along the way. Opposite the pegboard was a rickety bookshelf filled with engineering texts, nuts and bolts, screws and nails, and Mrs. Levine's still-broken radio, hand mixer, and blow dryer. Between them was the unfinished wood desk/worktable that Mr. Levine was currently crouching beneath as he picked up an assorted collection of computer chips.

Caramel Nut Bars

"Everything's fine!" Mr. Levine said. "I tried to pull something off the top shelf and had a little mishap. Do you mind—?"

Before he could finish his question, Yitz and Yaakov were on the floor fishing computer chips out of the dust bunnies piled under the desk and in the corners of the shed.

"Thanks," Mr. Levine said as he rose and brushed off his pants.

"What are you working on?" Yitz asked.

Mr. Levine gestured at the baby monitor and walkie-talkie set on his desk. "Oh, nothing really. I'm tinkering a little."

Yaakov picked up one of the walkie-talkies "Hey, I remember these! Yitz, didn't you get them for Chanukah last year?"

Yitz rolled his eyes. "Yeah, the *girls* bought them for me. Pooled their money as an apology for using up all the hot water or something. Never worked at all."

Mr. Levine nodded. "I thought maybe I could get them to work with the baby monitor. You know, make a three-way communication set for you boys." He looked around them, then glanced at the door. "Where's Avi?"

Yitz grunted.

Yaakov adjusted his yarmulke. "He had something to do at home."

"Hmm. Well, I need to see if I can get them all to operate on the same frequency. And if we can boost the signal a little, then maybe you could each have yours at home and talk to each other. All together..." Mr. Levine's voice trailed off as he looked from Yitz to Yaakov and back again. "All right, what happened?"

Yaakov recounted the cake fiasco. Hearing the story from his side only made Yitz angrier. Why did he have to have such obnoxious sisters?

Mr. Levine shook his head as he listened to the story. "Yes. The salt would act as an enhancer, intensifying the smell of the cake." He laughed. "Your sisters baked a picture-perfect disaster of a cake."

"They did it on purpose. They—"

Mr. Levine put up his hand to stop Yitz. "Now, wait just a minute. They have one week. One. Week. I repeat, one week to get all the baked goods completed in time for the bake sale. The advertising is up all over the city — thanks in part to you guys — and that means there's no pushing this off. If those girls are going to raise any money for the school, they don't have time to waste on rather funny — but time-consuming — pranks on their little brother."

"I'm not Rivkie's little brother. I'm eleven months *older*," Yitz muttered through gritted teeth.

Mr. Levine pulled three matching computer chips out of the box, then placed the box back on the top shelf. "I think you understand what I'm saying. I understand why they're accusing you, too. They have a point. We put away the groceries last night. Who's to say we didn't make a mistake?"

Yitz clenched his fists at his sides as he began to turn to the door. He didn't need this. He didn't need to be attacked, especially in his safe place. "I can't believe I'm hearing this. You're supposed to be on my side. My *only* ally in this house, and you're siding with *them*?"

"I'm not *picking sides* here," Mr. Levine said. "I would hope my kids — all of them — will always be on the same side."

"Then why do we have so many *girls*?" Yitz shot back.

Chaos in the Kitchen

Mr. Levine laughed. "I don't believe I had much to do with that decision," he said, pointing up. "And trust me, as your sisters get older, I feel the weight of our lot in this world as much as you do — if not more."

Yitz harrumphed.

"Remember, you will get married one day and move out and hopefully go on to have lots of sons. I will *always* be the father of five girls."

Standing beside Yitz, Yaakov was trying not to laugh. Unable to really lash out at his father, Yitz turned on his friend. "What are you smirking about? It's easy for you to be smug. You come from a home of three boys."

The words were out before he could stop them. The silence that followed as Yaakov's face paled made him regret his thoughtlessness more than any yelling could.

"Trust me. I would give anything to have a sister," Yaakov whispered. He turned to Mr. Levine. "I'm sorry, it's getting late, and Savta is going to be wondering what happened to me. I'm going to grab my books from your room, Yitz, and go. I— I can't wait to see the walkie-talkies when they're up and running."

Caramel Nut Bars

Yitz's shoulders sagged as he watched Yaakov go. All the heat had left him, like a crumpled hot-air balloon. Yaakov had lost his parents three years earlier in a terrible car crash. He would never have a sister because he no longer had parents.

Mr. Levine sat on his wobbly office chair and wheeled it to his desk. He picked up one of the walkie-talkies and a screwdriver. "It's a tough thing when we let anger get ahold of us. We know the buttons. We know the exact things to say to hurt those we're closest to — those we least want to hurt." Putting down the screwdriver, he pulled the two pieces of the walkie-talkie apart and examined the insides. "It's kind of like an out-of-control train — eventually, it'll jump the tracks."

Yitz bit his lip. He took a step toward the door and rocked back and forth on his feet. The crazy thing was, he hadn't even been angry at Yaakov.

And apparently, Mr. Levine knew it. "And when that happens, there's no stopping what it runs into."

"I should go after him," Yitz said, taking another step in the direction of the door.

Chaos in the Kitchen

Mr. Levine looked up for the first time since Yaakov had left and shook his head. "I think you should let him go. Cool yourself off first. Why don't you go shoot some hoops in the driveway? I think I'm onto something here."

Yitz stepped back toward the desk. He loved tinkering with his father. But one look from his father told him that now was not the time to join in. "Yeah. Maybe I will."

CHAPTER 10

ROCKY ROAD ICE CREAM

By the time Friday morning rolled around, Yitz felt terrible about the day before. There was an uncomfortable knot in the pit of his stomach, and he could barely finish his Cheerios. Pushing around the last soggy rings in his bowl of milk, Yitz tried to come up with a way to say sorry without making Yaakov feel even worse. Yitz sighed.

Mrs. Levine turned to the table, holding Yitz's

lunch bag. "Is everything okay?" she asked.

Yitz shook his head. "I said something horrible to Yaakov yesterday. I don't want him to be mad at me."

His mother smiled and seated herself across from Yitz at the table. "You know what the amazing thing about a friend is?"

He shook his head.

"They always understand. A friend is like family."

Thinking of Rivkie, Yitz wrinkled his nose.

Mrs. Levine laughed. "I know your sisters can be overwhelming at times. But remember last year when we went on that hike and you got lost?"

Yitz nodded.

"We were so worried when you and Rivkie wandered off the trail. The whole family searched and searched. Daddy and I were almost ready to call the rangers' station when we finally found you."

Yitz remembered his own fear. It had sat in the middle of his chest like a giant boulder. And he remembered Rivkie's fear. Her face was paler than his white Shabbos shirt.

Rocky Road Ice Cream

Together, they'd decided the safest thing to do was to stay where they were and wait for their parents to find them. So they sat down on a mossy old log and began to say *tehillim* that they remembered by heart. They were still huddled side-by-side when everyone came crashing through the woods and found them fifteen minutes later.

Together. That was how they had gotten through it.

Then they were caught up in hugs with the entire family, and the whole world seemed a little bit brighter.

Yitz looked at Mommy. "Maybe they're not so bad."

Mommy smiled. "Family and friends have their moments of both good and bad. They know us." She leaned forward and winked. "That means they love us, even if we have problems to fix."

"But how do I fix it?"

Mommy rose from her seat and returned to the counter. "I wish I had an easy answer." She turned back and looked at Yitz over her shoulder. "But, like anything worthwhile, there isn't one. Be honest and say you're sorry. I think you might find that he's already forgiven you. Now, off to school before you're late."

"Okay, okay." Yitz picked up his backpack and tossed it over one shoulder, trudging to the front door. As he left the kitchen, he glanced back. Mrs. Levine was watching his progress with a small smile. "Thanks, Mom," he said.

Her face lit up as her smile grew. "That's what I'm here for."

CHAPTER 11

HUMBLE PIE

itz walked to school on his own that morning. When he arrived, he ignored the calls of his friends in the yard and went straight to his class. Yaakov was right where he expected to find him: in the front row, at his desk, nose buried in a Chumash while his pen hovered over his notebook.

Yitz slid into the seat beside Yaakov. "Hey," he said.

Chaos in the Kitchen

As soon as Yaakov heard Yitz, his shoulders sagged. He closed and kissed his Chumash and turned to Yitz. "Hey."

The entire way to school, Yitz had thought about what he would say. He wanted to come out and say sorry right away. This was his best friend, Yaakov! But the second Yaakov turned to him and looked at him with those expectant eyes, all the thoughts in Yitz's head became a mixed-up jumble.

The words he had carefully crafted vanished; weird rambling came out of his mouth instead. "So, I have this friend and he has this problem, and he doesn't really know how to fix it."

Yaakov lifted a single eyebrow. "Oh?"

Yitz twisted his hands in his lap. He stared at a small groove in the desk in front of him that someone had made with a pen. How many times had they pressed with a blue pen back and forth to make a dent in something so hard? How many times would he mess up before he got rid of all the anger inside him?

"Well, he is trying. He talked to his dad, and he even talked to his mom. And they want to help him. But it can be really hard, and maybe he needs someone else to help him."

Humble Pie

Yaakov nodded, trying not to smile. "Well, y'know, friends are good at helping with things, too. Have you tried to help him?"

Yitz placed both elbows on the desk as his head dropped into his hands. "I tried! But I guess maybe I can't do it by myself."

"Let me help," Yaakov said.

Yitz looked up and leaned toward Yaakov. "Would you?"

Yaakov shrugged. "Why not?"

Then, suddenly, the words came back. All Yitz's nervousness and embarrassment vanished as the apology poured out of him. "I'm sorry, Yaakov. I wasn't thinking. I was so mean and thoughtless, and I need to be more careful, and I don't know why I said it." Yitz looked up and made eye contact with Yaakov for the first time since coming in. "I'm sorry."

"S'okay," Yaakov said before opening his Chumash again. "Do you understand the Rashi in the second *pasuk*?"

Yitz turned to the Chumash. The conversation was over. They were friends again, and Yitz felt like a rock had been lifted off his shoulders. It was good to have friends.

CHAPTER 12

S'MORES

No matter how hard Yitz tried, he couldn't keep his eyes forward and looking at the rebbe. He sat in his seat, turning sideways so his body faced Yaakov, while his gaze kept drifting to the back of the classroom. Avi was there, leaning back in his chair on two legs, in the last row of the class. Why had his friend abandoned them? And why hadn't the rebbe commented on the move?

S'mores

"Isn't that right, Avi?"

Startled by the sound of his name, Avi fell backward, landing with a thud on the back of his chair. Yitz tried to contain his smirk. But, a little bit, it felt like what should happen to someone who ditches his friends.

The rebbe took a step toward Avi. "Perhaps that isn't the safest way to daydream?"

Avi nodded as he gingerly got to his feet, rubbing his backside. "Sorry, rebbe," he said.

Yaakov caught Yitz's eye and frowned. There was something up with their friend, but Yitz had no idea how to find out what. He shook his head and shrugged. Way in the back, Avi turned away from them without his usual friendly wink and busied himself with righting his fallen chair.

When the bell rang for recess, Yaakov placed a hand on Yitz's arm to stop him from jumping up with the rest of the class. Once the room was empty, the two of them walked together to the back and stopped in front of Avi. Avi was casually flipping through a *Marshmallow* comic.

"Maybe it's time to let us in on what's going on with you?" Yitz asked, trying to keep the accusatory tone out of his voice.

With a sigh, Avi looked up. "You wouldn't understand," he said.

Yaakov slid into Eli B.'s vacated seat, while Yitz grabbed a seat in front of Avi and straddled it backward. "Why don't you try us?" Yaakov asked.

Avi shook his head and turned back to his comic. "I don't know what to say. You two always know everything. And I..." He shook his head. "My mom got me a tutor."

"What?" Yitz leaned forward. "That's great! My dad has to learn with me three times a week because I've been struggling with geometry. Everything was easy until they expected me to understand 3D shapes on a flat paper."

"But this is different," Avi said as he lowered his head onto his arm on the desk. "This is Chumash. It should be easy!"

"Why do you say that?" Yaakov shrugged. "Saba says everyone struggles in different areas. Look at me, I can't play sports like you and Yitz. We all have strengths and weaknesses."

Yitz felt things begin to fall into place. Strengths and weaknesses. That was a great way of looking at it. And if Yitz took what his mom had said, then the only way to get through the weak spots was together. Suddenly, his anger at Avi seemed silly. There was always an explanation.

"So that's where you were yesterday?" Yitz asked.

Avi nodded glumly. "I can't study with you because I have to study with him."

Yaakov shrugged. "No worries. We still haven't gotten our dessert for hanging up the posters. Hopefully today, after the game, the girls will have something yummy for us."

Yitz nodded. "Yeah, you were so lucky you didn't taste the disaster they prepared for us yesterday."

Yaakov laughed as Yitz recounted the story, and soon all three of them were chuckling.

Avi closed his comic book and looked at Yitz with big, round eyes. "You still want me at the game today?"

"Of course, we do! We don't stand a chance without your help. As Yaakov already said, he's not going to win it for us."

Yaakov nodded. "You cannot leave us with all those Elis."

Chaos in the Kitchen

"But—"

"No buts! Right, Yaakov?" Yitz turned to Yaakov for his agreement.

Yaakov clapped Avi on the back. "Avi, you're not getting rid of us that easily."

CHAPTER 13

MOLE PUDDING

itz stretched his arms out toward the two trees flanking him and took a deep breath. Most of the boys from Yitz's class were pressed in a corner at the other end of his yard. He stepped forward and crouched into his best goalie stance as he watched the ball careen toward him with the boys crashing after it.

The best time of year was that magical month when Fridays got longer but the school hadn't quite caught up to the calendar. On those golden days, school still ended early, but there was a whole long afternoon before Shabbos. Those afternoons were reserved for the most epic soccer tournaments ever to hit the fourth grade and Yitz's treeless backyard. Well, almost treeless. Two giant spruce trees stood guard on either end of the yard, perfectly spaced to make goal posts. Everyone was there. Sixteen boys perfectly divided into two slightly undersized soccer teams fighting it out in a game more intense than the World Cup.

Eli B. came up the middle and intercepted. Spinning, he kept the ball tight between his feet and started back up the field. Directly before him, Efraim stood, shuffling back and forth, preparing to move in. Before Efraim attacked, Eli B. kicked the ball to the side, to Eli C. As Shimmy and Motty moved in, the Elis continued to volley the ball back and forth. Eli C. to Yaakov, to Eli K. Then back to Eli B. Back to Yaakov — now Avi. Avi stopped the ball with the toe of his shoe and turned away from a charging Efraim. He dribbled the ball between his feet, moving closer to the other team's goal. Efraim slid in beside

Mole Pudding

Avi, making a grab with his left foot. At the last second, Avi kicked the ball to Eli B.

Yitz cracked his knuckles as the whole volley started again. Eli B. to Eli C. to Yaakov. Shimmy and Motty tried to close in again from the front as Efraim locked in the rear. The ball flew back to Eli K. He bounced it on his knee and got it back on the ground. To Yaakov — to Eli B. and back to Avi...who tripped and missed the ball. With a whoop, Efraim reclaimed the ball and ran toward Yitz.

Yitz bounced on the soles of his feet, watching the ball and his teammates. He moved from one side of the goal to the other, as Efraim wove easily between one stunned boy after another.

"Come on, Elis," Yitz called, "stop him!"

Three boys — all named Eli — looked up and waved at him. "We're trying!" the closest called before managing to kick the ball through Efraim's feet and back to the other end of the yard. Unfortunately, Shimmy was the one who stopped it, and the ball moved toward Yitz again.

Avi was still trying to regain his footing. Yaakov was tangled with Motty, and three Elis madly chased Shimmy toward the goal. Yitz moved forward, preparing to stop the ball, but it was no use. Shimmy kicked it high and in the corner. Yitz's best leap still only allowed his fingertips to brush the ball as it flew past him. Goal for the other team.

Shimmy ran back to his team's side of the yard with his arms in the air. He high-fived Efraim, fist-bumped Motty, and jumped onto Dov.

Yitz kicked the dirt at his feet, then went to retrieve the ball. Meanwhile, his dejected team trudged over to Avi.

"You cost us the game," Eli B. bellowed.

Avi cringed. "It was an accident. I think I stepped in a mole hole."

"One more thing to add to your list of failures," Eli K. spat.

Eli C. shook his head.

Yaakov put his hand on Avi's shoulder. "Any of us could have messed up like that."

"We should have won the game," said Eli C.

"I'm captain next week," Eli K. said, "and don't expect me to pick you, Avi."

"Hey, guys, lay off Avi, would you?" Yitz said as he joined his team. "We all mess up sometimes. We'll definitely win next week."

Mole Pudding

With some half-committal nods and a couple of shrugs, Yitz led his team to the center of the yard. One by one, each of them shook the hands of their opponents. "Have a great Shabbos, everyone," Yitz said. "Same time, same place next week, 'kay?"

The boys grabbed their discarded bags and sweaters from the porch and began to disperse. Soon, only Avi, Yaakov, and Yitz remained.

"I'm sorry about messing up the game."

Yaakov rolled his eyes. "It's usually me who messes up. This week was your turn."

After the whole craziness at school, Yitz didn't think Avi's ego could handle another beating. He swallowed his disappointment and smiled at his friend. "It's not the World Cup. We'll get them next week. Now I think my sisters should finally have something for us to taste that's edible."

Avi and Yaakov followed Yitz into the house. The smell of cookies permeated every corner. Yitz's mom had worked extra hard to make sure she had all the food ready for Shabbos by the time the girls had arrived home from school so that they could spend as much time baking as possible. And from the smell of it, things were off to a great start.

Avi rubbed his stomach. "All that exercise made me hungry. I think—"

But they didn't find out what he thought.

His words were drowned out by an earsplitting wail coming from the kitchen.

CHAPTER 14

TOFFE

itz reached the kitchen at the same time as Mrs. Levine. Rivkie stood by the oven, still screaming. "What—?" he began.

Before he could even finish his question, Rivkie had turned away from the oven and stormed toward him. "You!" she screeched.

Yaakov and Avi cowered behind Yitz. Yitz's eyes opened in surprise, and he stepped backward, right onto Yaakov's toes.

Chaos in the Kitchen

"You did this." Rivkie took another step toward him. "You think this is funny? Well, you can clean it up!"

Yitz shook his head. His mouth hung open, but no words came out as he spluttered against his sister's rage.

Meanwhile, Mrs. Levine had walked across the kitchen to the oven and was peering in at the cookie sheet with a funny expression on her face. "Rivkie, dear? What did you put in these cookies?"

Yitz followed his sister to his mother's side and looked over Rivkie's shoulder at the bubbling, gooey mess hardening on his mother's favorite cookie pan.

"I followed the recipe exactly as you gave it to me," Rivkie wailed. "I even checked the sugar to make sure it wasn't salt. I was so careful, and now look at this mess!"

Mrs. Levine walked to the pantry and pulled out the flour container. She twisted off the lid, stuck one finger inside, and licked the powder stuck to it. Then she nodded. "It's icing sugar."

Behind Yitz, Avi guffawed. Yitz elbowed him in the ribs as a warning. They had nothing to do with this. But seeing the humor in it was the exact behavior that would make Rivkie—

"I knew it!" She turned back to Yitz. "You! You did this. You and your goofy friends. You ruin everything."

"Now, Rivkie," Mrs. Levine said, "let's not make accusations like that."

A single tear escaped from Rivkie's right eye. "I asked Malkie. I checked with her because it seemed too fine to me. She said Daddy had probably bought cake flour to make baking easier. I know Yitz did this on purpose. He wants to ruin me." She hiccuped as more tears escaped her eyes. "He ruins everything."

Yitz stepped toward his mom and Rivkie. What ever happened to innocent until proven guilty? "That's not fair! I—"

But he didn't get to finish. With one more shudder and gasp, Rivkie turned away from him and ran up the stairs. Moments later, they heard the slam of her door. Startled and confused, Yitz was left speechless as Mrs. Levine glared down at him.

"Did you do it?" she asked.

"Why do you ask that as if you've already decided the answer?"

Chaos in the Kitchen

His mother shook her head. "Yitz, did you do it?"

The anger threatened to explode in Yitz. He felt it bubbling like a pot of soup. "What? She makes a mess and I'm to blame?"

Mrs. Levine took a deep breath and looked from one boy to the other. "I think it's time for your friends to head home."

Yaakov and Avi nodded and practically raced to the door with nothing more than a quick "Have a good Shabbos."

Yitz threw his hands up. "This is crazy. If they're leaving, I'm leaving, too," he yelled. And he ran from the house, slamming the front door behind him.

CHAPTER 15

TREACLE SPONGE

"Whoa, Yitz, whoa," Mr. Levine said as Yitz barreled straight into him as he was coming up the front steps.

Mr. Levine grasped Yitz's shoulders. His father's hands felt like ice that made boiling soup turn lukewarm. Yitz sagged to a seated position on the top step of the porch.

Mr. Levine tossed his jacket, hat, and brief-case onto a nearby chair and sat down beside his son. "Want to tell me what happened?"

Yitz leaned forward with his elbows on his knees and his chin cradled in his open palms. "Another mess in the kitchen, and Rivkie is blaming me again."

Mr. Levine cocked an eyebrow. "Can I ask what happened?"

"She used icing sugar in the cookies instead of flour."

Mr. Levine started to laugh. "That's great. Cookies without gluten or any binding substitute."

Yitz tried to keep his own laughter in check. "It spread into one giant cookie. Only, it looks more like a giant toffee, bubbling and spreading all over Mommy's favorite cookie sheet."

His father's laughter stopped. "It'll be quite the mess to clean up. Maybe we should help?"

"But I didn't do it!"

"And I believe you. Trust me, I certainly didn't do it either. I love my science experiments as much as the next guy, but a kitchen full of *girls* is not something any man wants to mess with."

Yitz leaned back and folded his arms against his chest. "Rivkie made the mess, let her clean it up. Maybe she did it herself to get me in trouble. I bet she knew all along it was icing sugar. She probably just didn't realize how much of a mess it would make."

Beside him, Mr. Levine was nodding with his words. "A possibility," he said.

And before he even continued, Yitz knew his dad was only being polite.

"But then, I wonder. Rivkie is expected to bring a lot of treats next week to the bake sale. Time is short." He counted on his fingers. "When you take out Shabbos, there are only three baking days left until the sale on Wednesday. Do you really think the girls would want to sabotage themselves and risk the anger of their whole school?"

Yitz scratched his head. "But someone did it."

Mr. Levine nodded. "And I think I know three boys who are pretty good at solving mysteries. Maybe the best thing to do is solve this mystery for the girls so they have someone to blame other than you."

Yitz shook his head. "But how can I figure out who did it? I'll need proof and suspects. And it wasn't me, and you already said it wasn't the girls. And you and Mommy didn't do it." Yitz shrugged. "I don't even know where to start."

His father stroked his beard as he leaned against the railing. "What we need is a way to keep an eye on what's happening in the kitchen."

"Like a video camera?"

Mr. Levine nodded. "Maybe. I'll talk to Mommy and the girls. Why don't you go to Yaakov or Avi's house until the girls cool down?"

Yitz bit his lip. He thought about Rivkie crying in her room and about Mommy's cookie sheet. Then he remembered the story his mom had reminded him of that morning. Levines stuck together. Yitz shook his head. "Thanks, Daddy. But I think I should go help Mommy clean up the mess."

CHAPTER 16

CHOCOLATE LAVA CAKE

itz woke up by himself on Sunday morning.

How odd.

Stretching his arms up to the ceiling, he glanced around the room. Chavie wasn't in her crib, so her crying hadn't woken him. His bed, amazingly, still had his blanket and pillow on it — so it wasn't that. Strange.

Shrugging, he quickly washed his hands in

the bowl beside his bed, then jumped up and looked out the window.

The entire neighborhood was still sleeping. So why was he awake? Shrugging again, he took a deep breath and stretched again. Then it hit him. The most overwhelming, delicious scent of chocolate cake.

After Wednesday's mix-up, Thursday's fiasco, and Friday's mess, Yitz wasn't getting his hopes up, but there was no reason to dawdle in his room. He dressed quickly and hurried down the stairs. Chavie and Shoshie blocked the path to the kitchen. Shoshie had lined up all her dolls in a row, with Chavie right in the middle. Each spot had a cup, plate, and fork in front of it, and Shoshie was moving up and down the line, giving each of her dolls a bite. Apparently, it was breakfast time for the dolls, too.

Rolling his eyes, Yitz stopped on the third step, grabbed the handrail on the wall, leaped into the air, and swung his feet in an arch over the tea party. He made it to the kitchen doorway, knocking over only one doll in the process.

As he celebrated his success, Shoshie did the opposite. "Hey! Be careful."

Chocolate Lava Cake

"Don't play by the stairs if you don't want people going by," Yitz tossed over his shoulder.

"But they're eating. I need to be next to the kitchen for that!"

Yitz bent down to eye level with his little sister. "It's just pretend," he whispered.

Shoshie slid back from her brother and jumped up. "Mommy!" she cried, running from the room.

Yitz rolled his eyes, patted poor, abandoned Chavie on the head, and turned back to the kitchen. Yitz was not going to let Shoshie ruin his good Sunday morning.

"You're up early," said Chaya Bracha as he walked into the kitchen.

Yitz shrugged. "Smells good. Time for breakfast."

Yitz slid behind his big sister and peeked over her shoulder at the chocolate cake cooling on the counter. "Looks amazing."

She nodded. "It tastes great, too. I double-checked all the ingredients before putting them in, and I tested some of the leftover bits when I took it out of the pan."

Yitz bobbed his head up and down. Better to be agreeable on such a good morning even if he didn't really care — as long as he got to try it, too. "When do I get some?" he asked, giving his most winning smile.

Chaya Bracha laughed — as sisters went, she really wasn't such a bad one. "Slow down, Yitz. I need to make the icing. I'm doing that next. Why don't you have a bowl of cereal while you wait, and let me work?"

It was a bright Sunday morning. There was good chocolate cake on the counter. Yitz had no interest in ruining it by fighting with the *girls*. He grabbed a bowl and spoon, and slid into his seat at the kitchen table, busying himself with choosing between Cheerios, Rice Krispies, and cornflakes.

"It's good to see you bright and early, but do you have to fight with Shoshie?"

Yitz looked up from his cereal mid-bite. The spoon hovered in the air until he remembered to drop it back into the bowl. Small droplets of milk splattered the tablecloth. His mother stood in the doorway to the kitchen, one arm cradling Chavie and the other holding a sniffling Shoshie's hand.

"She blocked the hallway and stairs."

Chocolate Lava Cake

Mrs. Levine placed Chavie in her high chair and strapped her in before giving her a handful of Cheerios. Then she picked up Shoshie and slid into a seat across from Yitz. Shoshie wiggled in their mother's lap, curling closer to her while glaring at Yitz.

"I wanted to get past, so I jumped. I barely touched anything."

"But you could have," Shoshie said.

Mrs. Levine brushed down Shoshie's big brown curls with her hand, shushing her. "I agree it's not the best place for her to play, but maybe we could have found a better way to solve this?"

"But, Mommy, I didn't say anything. I jumped. Had I tried walking through the maze of toys, I would have broken or knocked down even more."

Mrs. Levine kissed Shoshie's cheek and gently pushed her off her lap. "Shoshie, dear, why don't you go get your dolls, and you and I are going to find an even better place for you to play."

"But what if I need something from the kitchen? My babies can't wait that long. You don't make Chavie wait that long."

Chaos in the Kitchen

As if to prove Shoshie right, Chavie pointed at her sippy cup on the counter and started shrieking.

Sighing, his mother rose from her seat and went to rinse and refill the cup. She handed it to Chavie, who grabbed it and started sucking happily. "Shoshie," Mrs. Levine said, placing her hands on her knees and leaning forward, "let's ask Daddy when he gets home. Maybe he can think of a way for you to have your own kitchen in the den."

The front door opened and slammed. "Hello, girls!" Mr. Levine called from the entryway. "Oh! And you too, Yitz," he said, looking surprised as he walked into the kitchen. He clapped Yitz on the shoulder.

"Why is everyone making such a big deal of me being up?"

"Because you usually don't grace us with your presence until lunchtime on Sundays," Rivkie said as she pranced into the kitchen.

Yitz looked from his mom (trying not to smile) to his dad (shrugging) to each of his sisters (smirking or outright laughing). "This is not fair. Next time—"

But no one heard what would happen next time, because beside the stove Chaya Bracha was shrieking.

Their parents rushed forward as Chaya Bracha backed up, waving her hands, a wooden spoon still in her hand.

Yitz stood up and tried to see what was going on over Chavie's high chair. Was there a fire? A bug? His sisters had freaked out for much less. But this — this was much worse.

The small saucepan Chaya Bracha had been stirring moments before had bubbled up and over the sides. It splattered and sprayed most of the kitchen with a chocolatey, gooey mess. Mrs. Levine grabbed Chaya Bracha and pulled her away before the hot volcano of liquid burned either of them.

Mr. Levine leaned forward and turned off the stove. Next, he grabbed a glove from the counter, used it to shift the pot off the element, and dumped the mess into the sink. "Chaya Bracha, what was in there?"

Chaya Bracha was standing wrapped in Mrs. Levine's arms, sniffling. She lifted her head, revealing streaks of tears running down her cheeks. "I— I was just making icing. I d-don't understand."

Mr. Levine stepped up to the counter and scanned the ingredients scattered from one end to another. Picking up the container that said Icing Sugar, he stuck his pointer finger in, pulled it out with a brushing of powder, and stuck it in his mouth. His puckered lips and wrinkled nose said it all: the container didn't hold icing sugar. "Baking soda," he said.

Mrs. Levine rolled her eyes.

Rivkie and Malkie gasped.

And Yitz, unable to control himself while looking at his father's twisted face, guffawed.

Chaya Bracha pushed away from their mom and wiped her eyes. She turned toward the kitchen table with her finger pointed and wagging at Yitz. "You!"

The laughter washed away as Yitz jumped up, knocking over his chair. He lifted his hands in surrender and took small steps backward, toward the hallway and stairwell. "I didn't do it."

But Chaya Bracha kept coming. Behind her, Mr. and Mrs. Levine were too stunned at their always-calm oldest daughter's reaction to stop her. "I defended you. I told Rivkie she should leave you alone. But it was you all along, wasn't it?" She swatted at the tears still falling from her eyes. "Why would you do this?"

Yitz had misjudged the path to the door and ended up against the wall as his sister continued to step toward him. His eyes roved over the faces in front of him. His mom's disappointment, Rivkie's anger, Chaya Bracha's passionate look of betrayal, and finally, his dad's shocked disbelief. "It wasn't me," he told all of them.

On the stove, the remains of the chocolatey goop had finally stopped bubbling. It had pooled near the edge of the polished stainless-steel stovetop and was dripping onto the freshly cleaned off-white tiled floor. Each oversized drop fell like a bomb, exploding and splattering brown goop across the floor and onto the light-wood cabinets.

Mr. Levine locked eyes with his cornered son and gently shook his head. "Did you do it, Yitz?"

"I wouldn't have even known that would happen," Yitz said, gesturing to the mess. Then he bit his lip. His words sounded like an admission of guilt.

Chaos in the Kitchen

His father shook his head and turned to Mrs. Levine. "Why don't you take the girls out of here. I think they need a break from all their hard work. Yitz and I are going to clean this up."

Rivkie looked like she was about to protest, but one look from their mom and she snapped her mouth shut. Mrs. Levine grabbed Chavie while Malkie took Shoshie's hand, and all the girls filed out of the room.

CHAPTER 17

SPONGE CAKE

itz met his father's eyes as he stepped forward. "I really, honestly, truly didn't do it. You have to believe me," Yitz said as he looked at his father without blinking.

Mr. Levine watched Yitz, waiting. After a moment, Mr. Levine shook his head and looked away. "Why don't you go get a bucket of soapy water, and we can start cleaning up this mess?"

Yitz bowed his head and turned from the

room. This was not the time to argue. He could feel it, his anger, simmering right below the surface, asking to be let out. But he stayed in control. Freaking out at his father wasn't the answer.

He kicked the abandoned tea party out of the way as he moved through the hallway to the closet where they kept the bucket, broom, and mop. Grabbing the soap, he poured a generous dollop into the large green bucket before lugging the bucket and mop back to the kitchen.

Mr. Levine stood over the stove, spraying the sticky chocolatey goop with kitchen cleaner. He looked up as Yitz moved to the empty sink to fill the bucket. "I'm proud of you."

Pulling the nozzle out and down to the bucket, Yitz began filling the bucket. He watched the soap bubble as suds fizzed up the sides. "Oh?"

"You could have gotten angry. You could have screamed and yelled. Especially since you didn't do it. But you stayed calm. I know it's hard, and I'm proud."

Yitz swung the faucet handle back to the off position and let go of the nozzle, allowing it to snap back into place. He had wanted to scream and yell and tell his sisters everything he thought of them. But he had held back. Mostly, he had been too surprised at first to lash out. "I didn't get the chance to get angry. It's not that I controlled myself." He shook his head. "The whole thing was over before I even got mad. Once I was mad, they were gone."

His father waved a gloved finger at Yitz. "Don't discount your success," he said. "It was your cool head that made the fight end so quickly."

As Yitz dunked the mop in the sudsy water and began to clean the floor, he thought about his father's words. He hadn't reacted to their anger, so Rivkie and Malkie and Chaya Bracha had no one to fight with. They had stopped screaming and followed their mom without complaint. Maybe his father was right. "I guess anger is kind of like baking soda," Yitz said, sloshing the mop across the floor. "The more you pour in, the bigger the mess."

Mr. Levine laughed. "I think the question is how you're going to figure out who *did* do this?"

Yitz nodded. As he swung the mop back and forth, swirling the sudsy water until it turned brown with the sticky chocolate, he tried to devise a plan. Someone was messing up the pantry supplies when no one else was around. "We need a way to watch the kitchen," he said.

"Hmm." Mr. Levine stroked his beard.

Yitz's mind continued working. Watching needed eyes, and eyes meant— "Hey, what did Mommy say about putting up a camera?"

Mr. Levine shook his head. "Mommy said no."

Yitz sagged, leaning against the mop. From the other room, the sounds of Chavie giggling and Rivkie chattering gave him an idea. Of the five senses, two could be recorded from a distance: sight and sound. If they couldn't use one, maybe they should try the other? "Hey, Daddy, what happened to the baby monitor you were tinkering with?"

CHAPTER 18

PÍNEAPLE UPŚIÞ-DOWN CAKE

itz bounced the ball, lined up the shot, then...*swoosh*! Another three-pointer from above the foul line. Yaakov and Avi were due to arrive any minute, so Yitz had decided to shoot some hoops until they showed up. He dribbled toward the side of the basket, prepared, and jumped for a lay-up — and *boom*! The ball careened off to the left, landing in his mother's rosebushes.

Chaos in the Kitchen

Mr. Levine had canceled his Sunday schedule to finish up the walkie-talkie baby-monitor contraption. But he needed absolute silence when soldering. Sometimes Yitz was able to control his curiosity long enough to stay quiet, but not when he was being blamed for everything.

Yitz jogged over to the flower bed and fished out his basketball. He managed to grab it and roll it back without pricking himself on even one thorn.

The thorns in the kitchen were a different story. The girls had banned all non-bakers from the kitchen. When he had attempted to get a glass of water just a few minutes before, the dirty looks had left him shaking with anger. He had kept control so far this morning. But if he wanted that to continue, he needed to avoid the kitchen.

Another run while dribbling, this time from the left side. Set-up, jump, bang, swoosh! Success! Yitz grabbed the ball and dribbled back to the foul line. The improvement of his game was one more surprising bonus to keeping a lid on his anger.

Pineapple Upside-Down Cake

Line up, jump, and nothing but net! Loud applause and whoops from the street caused Yitz to fumble the returning ball as he spun to see his friends cheering from the sidewalk.

Yaakov ran to the rose bushes to fetch the ball. "Shouldn't you be studying?" he asked.

Yitz shrugged. "Nowhere to study. My mom's upstairs with the little girls making a racket, my dad's in the workshop tinkering, and the girls have banned me from any room even near the kitchen."

"They still think you did it?" Avi asked.

"Yes, and today's mishap was the worst." Yitz told his friends about the volcanic icing. "Can you believe they think I did that?"

Silence greeted Yitz's question. He looked from Yaakov to Avi and back again. Yaakov bit his lip, holding back a smile and avoiding eye contact. Avi grabbed the ball from Yaakov and nailed a lay-up of his own.

"You have to admit it's really hilarious," Avi said, catching the ball and then throwing it back at Yitz.

"But I didn't do it!"

Avi stared at Yitz, meeting his pleading eyes.

"Nah. You didn't. Only I have the brains in this threesome to come up with such a prank."

Yaakov rolled his eyes. "So the only thing left to do is prove your innocence."

Yitz dribbled the ball and nodded. "My dad is working on a plan."

Yaakov raised his eyebrows and glanced in the direction of the shed. "A plan?"

"Yeah. Remember that walkie-talkie thing he was working on? We're going to set it up in the kitchen and hopefully catch the saboteur red-handed."

Avi cocked an eyebrow. "Saboteur?"

Yitz shrugged again. "My dad's word, not mine. It means the guy doing sabotage or the one messing with the ingredients."

"Doesn't really matter what we call him." Yaakov tossed the ball onto the front porch. "We only need to stop him."

"You're right," Yitz said. "Let's see if my dad is done because none of us are getting chocolate cake until the saboteur is caught."

CHAPTER 19

CHOCOLATE-COVERED PRETZEL

"Just a minute, boys. One more minute."

Avi, Yitz, and Yaakov stood crowded around the open shed door. Mr. Levine, yarmulke askew and sleeves rolled to the elbows, sat on the rickety office chair, facing the desk. He waved a soldering iron over his head. "I only need to connect this one last wire to the receiver, and I think I may..."

As Yitz stepped back from the door, giving

his father a bit more space, he wondered if he should buy a sign for the shed door. "Do Not Disturb: Mad Scientist at Work."

"And now—" Mr. Levine leaned even closer to the table. Below him, the ancient office chair creaked in protest. "Done!"

Mr. Levine unplugged, then set down his soldering iron and spun in the chair to face the boys. He held up his latest, greatest, homemade secret spy device in his left hand. "Do you want to test it before I put Humpty Dumpty's shell back on?"

Yitz took the walkie-talkie, careful not to touch the wires on the back. He put it up to his mouth and spoke. "Testing? Testing?"

His voice crackled out of the baby monitor on the table.

"It works great here," Yaakov said, "but what's its range?"

"Great question, Yaakov," Mr. Levine said. "I haven't finished the other walkie-talkie, but they're meant for you guys to communicate. Think of it as your own private three-way cell-phone service. So the range needs to hit each of you at your homes — about five miles."

Chocolate-Covered Pretzel

Yitz looked at the walkie-talkie with new eyes. "Really? That's amazing, Daddy!"

Yitz's father smiled. "Anything for my boys."

"You know what this means?" Avi asked, turning to the other two.

"I can make sure you don't keep us waiting in the morning by waking you up half an hour earlier?" Yaakov responded.

"Ha! Funny. No. We can set up this monitor in Yitz's kitchen and listen in at school."

"During break and lunch time," Mr. Levine said.

"Right. Of course," the boys chorused.

"Well, sounds like you all have a plan. Let me get these finished off, and hopefully we can catch our—"

"Saboteur," they sang.

CHAPTER 20

RED VELVET CAKE

Monday mornings were hard enough. But Monday mornings with a test were most definitely the worst. Yitz hadn't gotten much studying done Sunday afternoon. He had tested the walkie-talkies with Yaakov and Avi.

Yaakov had insisted they walk all the way to school to see if it would work. It had, but none of them had been surprised. Yitz's father's inventions always worked. Then they went back to Yitz's house to set up the monitor.

So now, as Yitz picked at his scrambled eggs, he wondered if all the testing had really been the best use of his time.

"Break a leg," Mrs. Levine said as he left for school.

"I feel queasy," Avi said as they walked to the corner to meet Yaakov and head to school.

Yitz clapped Avi's shoulder. "You got this. And even if not, I'm sure the rebbe will let you make up the marks."

Avi shrugged, and Yitz decided to stay quiet. Before, Yitz's anger would have pushed him to make Avi see things his way. But something was different. There was no need to fight.

Once seated in class, Yitz looked across the aisle to his two friends and gave a tiny thumbs-up. "We got this," he mouthed.

Yaakov nodded and returned the sign, then nudged Avi. "You're ready. Do your best."

"You sound like my mom."

Yitz glanced at the rebbe, then leaned forward. "If I was allowed, I'd help you. But the truth is, I don't think you need it," he said to Avi, winking.

Chaos in the Kitchen

Avi was about to answer when the rebbe walked up the aisle, motioning Yitz back into his seat. He smiled at them, then placed the tests on the desks face down.

"And we're starting now," the rebbe said. "You have one hour."

The rustling of papers around him told Yitz that everyone was rushing to begin. Slowly, he flipped over his paper, but he wasn't looking at it, he was looking at Avi. As Avi glanced at the first page, his shoulders relaxed, and a smile crossed his face. Then Avi leaned forward and began to write.

It was in the bag. Yitz grinned and began to fill in his own test.

"Ten minutes, guys," the rebbe said.

Yitz glanced up at the clock. One more question and ten minutes. Paced perfectly. It had taken him a few months to master it, but he had finally gotten his father's key to test success. Around him, there were two types of boys. Yaakov and Avi were whispering and trying not to disrupt him. Other boys who had finished earlier were reading a book or doing much the same. The other half of the class scribbled madly with pinched faces and tense shoulders. He could do this. One question he could finish without a problem—

Crackle, crackle, hiss.

The rebbe looked up sharply from his Mishnah in search of the sound.

Crackle. "Come here, Shoshie, we need more—" Hiss. Hiss.

It was coming from Yitz's backpack. The entire class stared at him, as his bag continued to spit out the sounds of two little girls playing.

Hiss. "Tova, I want to mix it now!" Crackle. "It's my turn to choose." Crackle. Hiss.

The rebbe rose from his seat and took a step forward. "Yitz, what's going on?"

Yitz opened his mouth, but nothing came out. He had forgotten to turn off the walkie-talkie before class.

Yaakov jumped up from his seat, waving his hand at the rebbe. "I need a bathroom pass, please."

Distracted by his star student, the rebbe turned back to his desk to get the hall pass.

Chaos in the Kitchen

Yaakov grabbed Yitz's still-crackling bag, called out, "Thank you!" to the rebbe and ran from the room.

Now that the class was silent again, the rebbe forgot the disruption and returned to his seat. Yitz heaved a sigh of relief. Yaakov had saved them again.

Yitz turned back to the one unfinished question on his test. Suddenly, he found himself scribbling madly like the others. He pinched his lips, and his shoulders were tense. The sooner he finished, the sooner they could get out of class and see what was happening at home.

A quick glance at Avi told him that his thoughts were the same. Tova was Avi's little sister. Mrs. Levine babysat her when Avi's mom was at work. And from the sound of it, Shoshie and Tova had a lot of explaining to do.

CHAPTER 21

GINGERBREAD MAN

When the last test was handed in, the rebbe let the class go to lunch. The boys had a thirty-minute break. Normally, they stayed at school. It wasn't worth it to run home, only to turn right back around and dash back to school. But today was different. Today, the boys would catch a saboteur.

In record time, Avi, Yitz, and Yaakov arrived at the Levine house. The three of them pushed open the front door, gasping for breath.

"Yitz! What are you doing home?" Mrs. Levine asked from the entrance to the kitchen.

The boys stood bent over in the entrance, panting, with their hands on their knees. None of them were able to speak. Trying to calm his racing heart, Yitz took three big gulps of air. He held up his finger to ask his mother to wait. She stood, watching the boys, with a dish towel and plate in her hand, trying not to laugh.

"Where...is...Shoshie?" Yitz finally spluttered.

"Why?" Mrs. Levine looked from one boy to the other. "She's with Tova. They set up their dolls by the stairs."

Yitz straightened and locked eyes with his mom. "They did it."

Mrs. Levine laughed and shook her head. "Did what? What can three big boys like you want from two little four-year-old girls?"

Yaakov recovered. With one last deep breath, he spoke. "Mrs. Levine, they didn't mean to, but we heard them."

"Shoshie and Tova are the saboteurs," Avi finished.

Gingerbread Man

Mrs. Levine crossed her arms over her chest and frowned. "Impossible."

Yitz stepped around his mom and into the kitchen. The pantry door stood ajar, and the sounds of Shoshie and Tova playing could be heard from the hallway. "Come, Mommy. We'll show you."

Shoshie's big curls were tucked up under one of Mrs. Levine's old snoods. Beside her, Tova was measuring a soft white powder into a tiny pink teaspoon. All the dolls were arranged in a circle around them, the same way Yitz had seen them on Sunday. How had he not figured it out then?

Mrs. Levine took in the two girls and the dolls. She glanced at the three overflowing pareve bowls from the kitchen. She kneeled in the kitchen doorway, careful not to knock over any of the dolls. "Shoshie? Tova? What are you doing, sweeties?"

Shoshie looked up and smiled a big toothy grin at her mom. Her dimples puckered as her eyes lit up. "We're feeding our babies lunch. Don't worry, Mommy, we only take a little bit. We fill the bowls, so we have enough. But we always put them back when we're done."

Tova nodded. "Yep, uh-huh. Back where we found it."

Mrs. Levine sagged against the frame of the door. "Shoshie, sweetie, you need to ask before taking something from the kitchen next time, okay?"

Shoshie frowned, and her eyes got squinty. "But I need to feed my babies, and you were busy with Chavie."

Mrs. Levine smiled at Shoshie and patted her on the head as she stood back up. "Okay."

The boys backed up into the kitchen, allowing Yitz's mother to enter. She dropped into the nearest seat at the table. "Looks like a lot of people — including me — owe you an apology, Yitz."

Yaakov began to pace. "Amazing. The saboteur wasn't a saboteur at all. Just a couple of girls who borrowed some stuff and didn't remember where to put it back."

"Doesn't help that they can't read," Avi said.

"But, really, it's my fault." Mrs. Levine sighed. "I should have noticed what they were doing."

Yitz shook his head. "Mommy, how could you have known they had gotten so creative with their food? None of the other girls ever did this sort of thing."

Mrs. Levine nodded. "You're right, Yitz. Thank you. But if you'll excuse me, I'm calling Daddy and getting him to make Shoshie her own kitchen as soon as possible. I think you three had better run back to school, or you'll be late."

CHAPTER 22

JUST DESSERTS

Streamers and twinkle lights lined the field of the Bais Yaakov school. Each of the sixteen classes had set up two tables of delicious desserts. In the center, tables with drinks and enough seating for the whole community appeared to be bursting at the seams. Everyone was there.

And *everyone* agreed that the Levine desserts on the tables of Chaya Bracha's, Malkie's, and

Just Desserts

Rivkie's classes were the tastiest reason to be there.

Seated at a table near the edge of the field, Avi, Yitz, and Yaakov had to stand on their chairs to see when the principal cleared her throat and asked for everyone's attention. As soon as she had relative quiet, she began to speak. "Thank you for joining us at the twenty-third annual Bais Yaakov Bake Sale. I don't want to keep you long from your sumptuous snacks, so I'll keep this short.

"Every year, the school runs a bake sale to help raise much-needed funds. This year, our girls decided to improve the library with the proceeds of this event.

"I am happy to announce that we have surpassed our goal. This means that not only have we raised enough money to buy new books for the library, we also have money to fund an extra field trip for the girls! Congratulations! You all deserve to have your cake and eat it, too."

Cheers and squeals from the girls of the Bais Yaakov school made Avi cringe. Yitz covered his ears, and Yaakov hid under the table. When the decibel level had returned to normal and Yaakov had come out of hiding, Yitz looked up to find the *girls* standing over him.

"Looks like you did it even with all the mishaps."

Chaya Bracha smiled as she glanced from Yitz to his friends. "And it seems we have you guys to thank for that."

Avi leaned back in his chair and kicked his feet onto the table. "All in a day's work," he said, before tipping all the way back and falling to the ground.

Yaakov tried not to laugh at Avi and looked at Chaya Bracha instead. "We're glad we could clear Yitz's name."

All three girls fidgeted in their place. Then Rivkie stepped forward as Malkie nudged her in the back. "About that," Rivkie said, "Yitz, I'm really sorry for jumping to conclusions."

As Avi righted his chair, Yitz slouched down and crossed his arms. "It wasn't fair, you know," Yitz said.

Malkie frowned. "You weren't being so levelheaded yourself. That sure makes someone look guilty."

Just Desserts

Yitz felt all the red-hot anger of their accusations against him bubbling beneath the surface. He glanced at Avi, who gave a small shake of the head. On his other side, Yaakov squeezed his arm. He could keep it in check with his friends behind him.

His sisters were trying to apologize. Even if they were doing a bad job of it, shouldn't he forgive them? He took a deep breath and pushed the anger away. "It's okay. Thanks for apologizing. I know it looked bad when I got all mad; I'm just glad we discovered the truth in time."

Chaya Bracha beamed at Yitz. Malkie winked, and Rivkie said, "You should know by now, we Levines can get through anything—"

"—As long as we stick together," Yitz finished.

Beside Yitz, Avi was finally back in his seat and leaning again. "Now, girls," Yitz said, "about those samples...?"

ACKNOWLEDGMENTS

hank you to all the children in my life. My own, my nieces and nephews, my cousins, and the children of my friends. Keep dreaming, keep growing, and keep up the crazy antics so that I have something to write about!

Thank you to my supportive family: my Mom, the Chelskys, Sumner Toronto, Sumner Rechovot, Buby Shoshana, the Dalys, the Indigs, and, of course, Sumner Kiryat Sefer.

Chaos in the Kitchen

Thank you to everyone at Menucha Publishers for once again doing such a good job. A special thank you to Anael Achituv for bringing Avi, Yitz, and Yaakov to life.

Lastly, I thank the Eibeshter for giving me the gift of words.

ABOUT THE AUTHOR

Sara Sumner is the author of *Wherever You Are* (Menucha Publishers, 2020). When she isn't writing, she can be found baking (successfully!), ironing her children's bead creations (but not their shirts!), or off on adventures with her family in Kiryat Sefer, Israel.

More great reads for kids from MENUCHA

BY ELLEN ROTEMAN

THE CASE OF THE DISAPPEARING CHANUKAH CANDLES

Mrs. Rabinovitz lives all alone, so no one else could have moved the candles. And if someone stole them, wouldn't other things be missing too?

Eleven-year-old Shimmy Stern has a knack for solving mysteries. When Mrs. Rabinovitz's Chanukah candles go missing, Shimmy and his siblings — the Five Star Detectives — snap on their plastic gloves and dust for fingerprints, decode tricky messages, and grill unwilling suspects. Will they find the candle culprit before Chanukah?

THE CASE OF THE UNFAIR SCIENCE FAIR

It's awful seeing my friends looking like they can't trust each other.
"Mr. Kessler?" I raise my hand. "I can solve the mystery of where things are going."

When items needed for their science projects disappear one by one, Shimmy's classmates are shocked — and suspicious. Will Shimmy and his siblings nab the thief and find the stolen goods before other classmates are unfairly accused?

More great reads for kids from MENUCHA

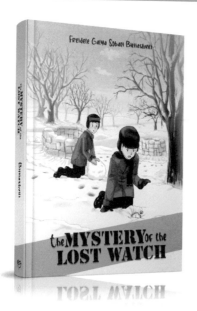